BoDiggety

Xray

Ozlo

Oola

Chip

Iota

Zolo is a zippy-zappy, oh-zo-happy, kooky-crazy,
oopsy-daisy, okey-dokey state of mind. A world where all things
squiggly wiggly, knobby blobby, square and round, plain or
spotty can all come together as one, and the results can be ah-mazing!
It's everything you can imagine...

ZOLO·A·B·Z

an alphabet book

written & illustrated by

byron glaser & sandra higashi

HARRY N. ABRAMS, INC., PUBLISHERS

OzLo

has something he wants
you to see! Starting with
A and ending with Z.

Aa

lphabet antics are all around, up in the air and down on the ground!

Bb

Big bulgy eyeballs in the pitch-black of night

are beautiful beings in the bright daylight!

razy cat coconuts! Cock-a-doodle-doo!

Dd

Ding-Dong!

ancing daisy doodles, a dizzy doggy too!

Ee

Express yourself! Roll your eyes and flap your ears!

Everybody, everywhere, eighty-eight cheers!

Ff

Flip-flop flying fish float in the sea!

A flock of flamingos frolic fancy-free!

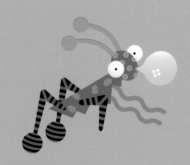

Gross and gooey glob of grape gum

GRRR!

7

gets Ozlo grumpy, gloomy, and glum!

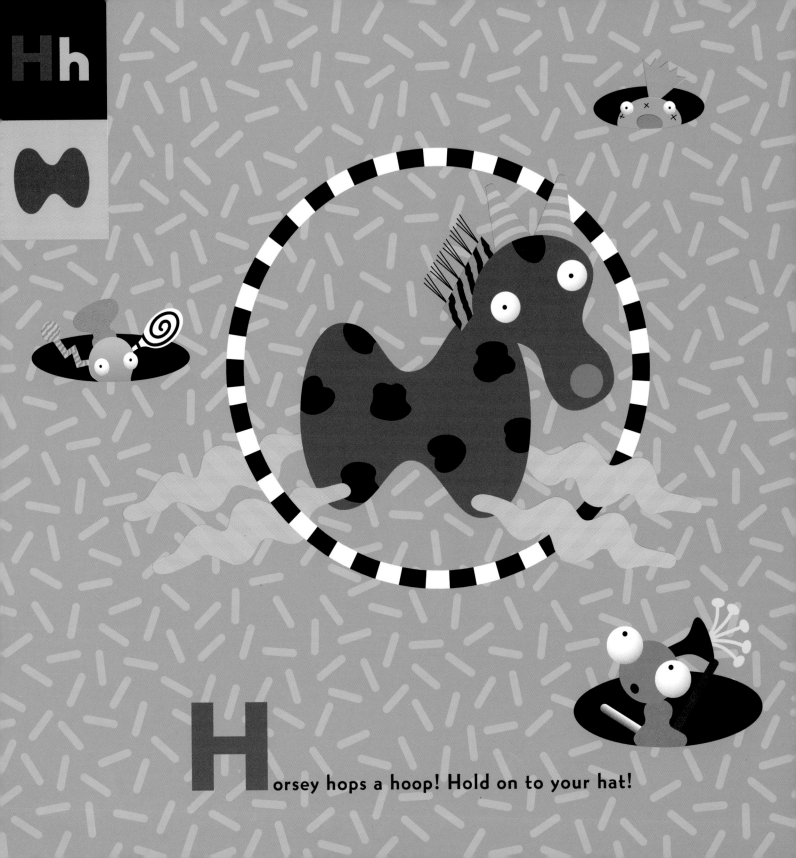

Hh

Horsey hops a hoop! Hold on to your hat!

I i

I cky ink is everywhere! Imagine that!

India Ink

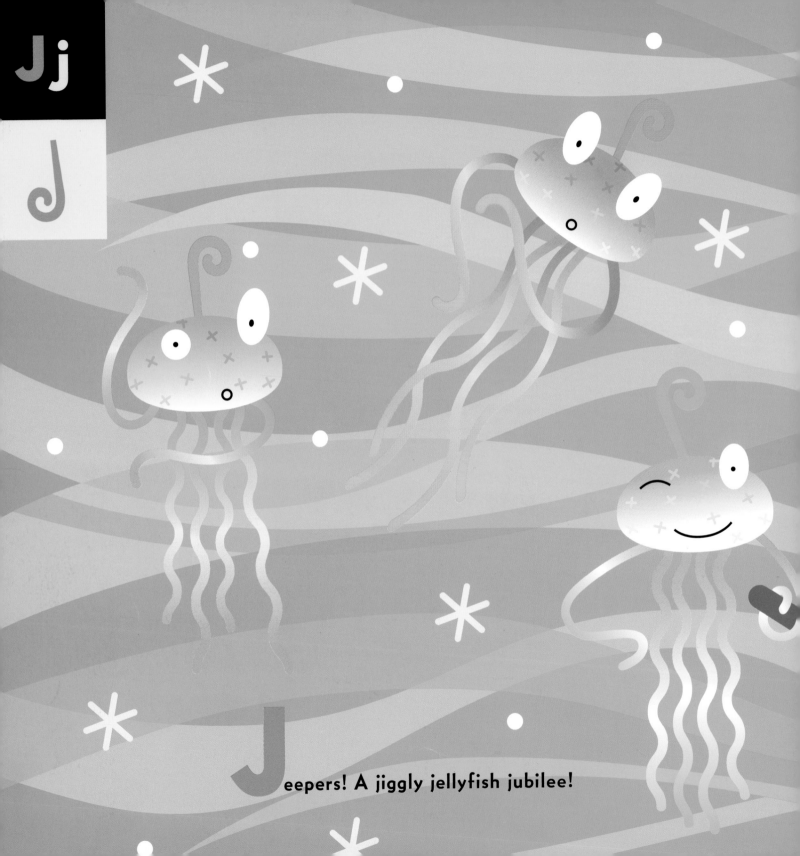

Jj

J

Jeepers! A jiggly jellyfish jubilee!

Ozlo jumps and juggles joyfully!

Kk

KINGSIZE Ketchup

KIDNEY BEANS

Kangaroos in the kitchen keep kidding around!

KABLAM!

Kicking kippers and kiwis onto the ground!

Ll

Love Land

ollipops! Lemon drops! Laughter and love!

arshmallows, monkey bars, the moon up above!

Nn

No Ozlo. Nope. Nothing. Nada. Nil.

range octopus oogles! Oops! Ozlo, be still!

Pp

Please plunge in! Pool party's begun!

Pizza, pretzels, popcorn, and plenty of fun!

Qq

the QUIRKY QUIZ Show

"uick question, Ozlo," queried the Queen.

WHO'S THE RASCAL?

1

2

3

"**R**odent or reptile—who's rotten and mean?"

Ss

S

Scoot and skate, ski and slide on slushy slopes of snow!

emperature's hot as a teapot, Ozlo's ready to blow!

p, up, upside down, over, under, through.

Uu

Vertical, vertigo—but oh, what a view!

Ww

Wacky, wild, wonderful world! Woo-wee!

Whatever you wish, you just might see!

X ray department

ray shows an exciting new view! All the letters are inside of... ou!

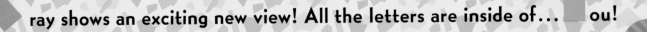

ZOLO

Zz

Zebra zooming! Zeppelins zip! What's Z reason for Z zany trip?

ZoLO!

Everything you can imagine,
and zillions more! With your
ABZ's, you can open any door!
So put letters together,
sound them out, have some fun.
Soon you can spell anything
under the sun!

A•B•Z things to find

Aa
acrobats
airplane
anteater
antelope
ants
apple
arrow

Bb
ball
balloon
bat
bee
beetle
blackbird
bluebird
boy
bug
butterfly

Cc
cactus
cake
candy
cat
cheese
chick
chocolate
clock
coconut
cookies
cotton candy
cowboy
croissant

Dd
daisies
dog

doll
doodles
dots
doughnuts
duck

Ee
eagle
ears
earth
éclair
eel
egg
eggplant
eight ball
elephant
elf
emu
extraterrestrial
eyeglasses
eyes

Ff
fans
feather
Ferris wheel
fireflies
fireworks
flamingos
flowers
flying fish
forest
french fries
frog
fudge

Gg
giraffe
goose
grape gum
grasshopper

Hh
hats
holes
hoop
horse

Ii
ice cream
ink blots
inkwell
insects

Jj
jelly beans
jellyfish
juggling
jump rope

Kk
kangaroos
ketchup
kettle
kidney beans
kippers
kitchen
kiwis

Ll
ladybug
lemonade

lemon drops
licorice
lizard
lollipops

Mm
macaroni
marshmallows
maze
meteor
monkey bars
monkeys
moon
mouse
mushroom

Nn
nada
nil
no
nothing

Oo
octopus
otter
oysters

Pp
palm trees
peacock
peanuts
penguin
pillow
pizza
plaid
pool

popcorn
pretzels
punch

Qq
Queen
question mark

Rr
rabbit
rat
rattlesnake

Ss
skates
skis
sled
snow
snowboard
squirrel
star

Tt
target
teapot
telescope
ten
thermometer
thirty
twenty
two-hundred-
fifty

Uu
umbrella
unicorn
unicycle

Vv
violets
violin
vultures

Ww
walrus
waterfall
water lilies
watermelons
weeds
whale
wheat
wildflowers
wind
windmill
wolf
woodpecker
worm

Xx
X chromosome
X ray

Yy
Y chromosome
yarn ball
yellow jacket
yo-yo

Zz
zebras
zeppelin
zigzag
zinnias
Zolo
zucchini

Dedicated to Tami and Johnny without whom there would be no A•B•Z's.
Very special thanks to our partner and friend Debbie Hirschfield, who inspires us
and who, along with Omri, Eden, and Avery, keeps us on track.

You may learn more about Zolo and Higashi Glaser Design at www.zolo.com

Design: Byron Glaser & Sandra Higashi
Production Manager: Hope Koturo

Library of Congress Cataloging-in-Publication Data
Glaser, Byron.
The Zolo A-B-Z book / by Byron Glaser and Sandra Higashi.
p. cm.
ry: Each letter of the alphabet is illustrated with zany Zolo toy characters.
ISBN 0-8109-4260-7
[1. Toys—Fiction. 2. Alphabet.] I. Higashi, Sandra. II. Title.
PZ7.G4804Zo 2003
[E]—dc21

2002012541

Printed and bound in China

10 9 8 7 6 5 4 3 2 1

HARRY N. ABRAMS, INC.
100 FIFTH AVENUE
NEW YORK, N.Y. 10011
www.abramsbooks.com

Abrams is a subsidiary of
LA MARTINIÈRE
GROUPE

BoDiggety

Boo

Oola

Ozlo

Buggy